Marx Abbott Hardy Defoe Melville Montaigne Machiavelli Haggard Chesterton Cooper Emerson Joyce Austen Hugo Eliot Grimm Stoker Carroll Christie Wilde Maupassant Molière Byron Schiller Engels Garnett Einstein Fitzgerald Hawthorne Smith Kafka Goethe Dostoyevsky Cotton Baum Kipling Doyle Hall Willis Leslie Dumas Henry Nietzsche Flaubert Turgenev Balzac Stockton Vatsyayana Crane Burroughs Verne Curtis Tocqueville Whitman Gogol Vinci Homer Widger Tolstoy Busch Darwin Thoreau Potter Freud Zola Twain Plato Scott Lawrence Kant Jowett Stevenson Dickens Andersen Cervantes Burton Hesse Harte London Descartes Poe Aristotle Wells Voltaire Hale James Hastings Cooke Bunner Shakespeare Richter Chambers Irving da Doré Swift Dante Chekhov Shaw Wodehouse Benedict Alcott Pushkin Newton

tredition®

tredition was established in 2006 by Sandra Latusseck and Soenke Schulz. Based in Hamburg, Germany, tredition offers publishing solutions to authors and publishing houses, combined with worldwide distribution of printed and digital book content. tredition is uniquely positioned to enable authors and publishing houses to create books on their own terms and without conventional manufacturing risks.

For more information please visit: www.tredition.com

TREDITION CLASSICS

This book is part of the TREDITION CLASSICS series. The creators of this series are united by passion for literature and driven by the intention of making all public domain books available in printed format again - worldwide. Most TREDITION CLASSICS titles have been out of print and off the bookstore shelves for decades. At tredition we believe that a great book never goes out of style and that its value is eternal. Several mostly non-profit literature projects provide content to tredition. To support their good work, tredition donates a portion of the proceeds from each sold copy. As a reader of a TREDITION CLASSICS book, you support our mission to save many of the amazing works of world literature from oblivion. See all available books at www.tredition.com.

Project Gutenberg

The content for this book has been graciously provided by Project Gutenberg. Project Gutenberg is a non-profit organization founded by Michael Hart in 1971 at the University of Illinois. The mission of Project Gutenberg is simple: To encourage the creation and distribution of eBooks. Project Gutenberg is the first and largest collection of public domain eBooks.

The Village Wife's Lament

Maurice Henry Hewlett

Imprint

This book is part of TREDITION CLASSICS

Author: Maurice Henry Hewlett
Cover design: Buchgut, Berlin – Germany

Publisher: tredition GmbH, Hamburg - Germany
ISBN: 978-3-8472-3277-3

www.tredition.com
www.tredition.de

POETICAL WORKS OF MAURICE HEWLETT

A Masque of Dead Florentines
Pan and the Young Shepherd: a pastoral
Artemision
The Agonists: a trilogy
Helen Redeemed and other Poems
Gai Saber: Tales and Songs
The Song of the Plow
Peridore and Paravail
The Village Wife's Lament

THE VILLAGE WIFE'S LAMENT

BY

MAURICE HEWLETT

CONTENTS

I

i

O what is this you've done to me,
Or what have I done,
That bare should be our fair roof-tree,
And I all alone?
'Tis worse than widow I become
More than desolate,
To face a worse than empty home
Without child or mate.

'Twas not my strife askt him his life
When it was but begun,
Nor mine, I was a new-made wife
And now I am none;
Nor mine that many a sapless ghost
Wails in sorrow-fare—
But this does cost my pride the most,
That bloodshedding to share.

Image of streaming eyes, tear-gleaming,
Of women foiled and defeat,
I am like Christ shockt out of dreaming,
Showing His hands and feet;
Showing His feet and hands to God,
Saying, "Are these in vain?
For men I have trod the sorrowful road,
And by them I am slain."
[Pg 7]
Seeing I have a breast in common,
I must share in that shame,
Since from the womb of some poor woman
Each evil one came—
Every hot and blundering thought,
Every hag-rid will,

And every haut king pride-distraught
That drove men out to kill.

A woman's womb did fashion him,
Her bosom was his nurse,
And many women's eyes are dim
To see their sons a curse.
Had I the wit some women have
To one such I would say,
"Think you this love the good Lord gave
Is yours to take away?"

O Hand divine that for a sign
Didst bend the rose-red bow,
Betokening wrath was no more Thine
With man's Cain-branded brow—
What now, O Lord, shouldst Thou accord
To such a shameful brood?
A bow as crimson as the sword
Which men have soakt in blood.

ii

I cannot see the grass
Or feel the wind blowing,
But I think of brother and brother
And hot blood flowing.
[Pg 8]
The whole world akin,
And I, an alien,
Walk branded with the sin
And the blood-guilt of men.

And often I cry
In my sharp distress,

It were better to die
Than know such bitterness.

iii

The Lord of Life He did ordain
How this world should run,
That Love should call thro' joy and pain
Two natures to be one;
Now jags across the high God's plan
Division like a scar,
For this is true, that He made man,
But man made war.

Had men the dower of teeth and claws
And not a grace beside them?
Were they given wit to know the laws
And hard hearts to outride them?
What drove them turn the sweet green earth
Into a puddle of blood?
What drove them drown our simple mirth
In salt tear-flood?

Has man been lifted up erect,
A lord of life and death,
His world's elect, and his brow deckt
With murder for a wreath?
What shall be done with such an one,
And whither he be hurl'd?
The Lord let crucify His Son—
Who gibbetted His world?

[Pg 9]

iv

Be it Pole Star or Southern Cross
That shelters me or you,
The same things are gain and loss,
And the same things true:
The home-love, the mother-love,
The old, old things;
The lad's love of maiden's love
That gives a man wings,

And makes a maid stand still, afraid
Lest it were all a dream
That he do think himself apaid
If she be all to him.
The arching earth has no more worth
Than this, to love, to wed,
To serve the hearth, to bring to birth,
To win your children's bread.

v

The bee pills nothing for himself,
Loading with gold his thigh,
The martin twittering, at his shelf,
Glancing from the sky
Not greedy ease make slaves of these;
Nor yet endures the cow,
Her failing knees and agonies
For price of joy I vow.
[Pg 10]
A call above the spell of love,
A crying and a need

To make two one, the fruit whereof
To nurture and to feed;
To brood, to hoard, to spend as rain
Virtue and tears and blood;
To get that you may give amain—
Of such is parenthood.

vi

I chose a heart out of a hundred
To nest my own heart in;
To have that plunder'd, and two hearts sunder'd—
Who had heart for the sin?
What woman's son that saw but one
Such sanctuary waste
Could set his lips like ironstone
And raven broadcast?

What harm did we to any man
That now I must moan?
We did but follow Nature's plan
And cleave to our own;
For Life it teaches you but this:
Seek you each other;
Rise up from your clasp and kiss,
A father and a mother.
[Pg 11]
O piety of hand and knee,
Of lips and bow'd head!
O ye who see a soul set free—
Free, when the heart is dead!
There is no rest but in the grave;
Thither my wasted eyes
Turn for the only home they have,

Where my true love lies.

There alongside his clay-cold corse
I pray that mine may rest;
I'll warm him with my lover's force
And feed him at my breast:
I'll nurse him as I nurst his child,
The child he never saw,
The stricken child that never smil'd.
And scarce my milk could draw.

Poor girls, whose argument's the same
For seeking or denying,
Who kiss to shield yourselves from blame,
And kiss for justifying;
How am I better now or worse,
Beguiler or beguiled,
Who crave to nurse a clay-cold corse,
And kiss a dead child?

vii

O I was shap't in comeliness,
My face was fashion'd fair,
My breath was sweet, I used to bless
The treasure of my hair;
A many prais'd my body's grace,
And follow'd with the eye
My faring in the village ways,
And I knew why.
[Pg 12]
Love came my way, fire-flusht and gay,
Where I did stand:
"This is the day your pride to lay
Under a true man's hand."

I bow'd my head to hear it said
In words of long ago;
For ever since the world was made
Our lot was order'd so.

And I was bred in pious bed,
Brought up to be good:
Respect yourself, my mother said,
And rule your own mood.
Fend for yourself while you're a may,
And keep your own counsel,
And pick at what the neighbours say
As a bird picks at groundsel.

But Love said Nay to Watch and Pray
When the birds were singing,
And taught my heart a roundelay
Like the bells a-ringing;
And so blindfast I ran and cast
My treasure on the gale—
Would the storm-blast had snapt the mast
Before I fared to sail!

[Pg 13]

II

i

Now that the Lord has open'd me
The evil with the good,
I am as one wise suddenly
Who never understood.
I see the shaping of my days
From the beginning,
When, a young child, I walkt the ways
And knew nought of sinning.

I see how Nature ripen'd me
Under sun and shower,
As she ripens herb and tree
To bud and to flower.
As she ripens herb and tree
Unto flowering shoot,
So it was she ripen'd me
That I might fruit.

I see—alas, how should I not,
With all joy behind?—
How that in love I was begot
And for love design'd.
Consentient, my mother lent,
Blessing, who had been blest,
That fount unspent, my nourishment,
Which after swell'd my breast.

[Pg 14]

ii

I learned at home the laws of Earth:
The nest-law that says,
Stray not too far beyond the hearth,
Keep truth always;

And then the law of sip and bite:
Work, that there may be some
For you who crowd the board this night,
And the one that is to come.

The laws are so for bird and beast,
And so we must live:
They give the most who have the least,
And gain of what they give.
For working women 'tis the luck,
A child on the lap;
And when a crust he learn to suck,
Another's for the pap.

iii

I know 'tis true, the laws of Life
Are holy to the poor:
Cleave you to her who is your wife,
Trust you in her store;
Eat you with sweat your self-won meat,
Labour the stubborn sod,
And that your heat may quicken it,
Wait still upon God.
[Pg 15]
Hallow with praise the wheeling days
Until the cord goes slack,
Until the very heartstring frays,
Until the stiffening back
Can ply no more; keep then the door,
And, thankful in the sun,
Watch you the same unending war
Ontaken by your son.

iv

Who is to know how she does grow
Or how shapes her mind?
The seasons flow, not fast or slow,
We cannot lag behind.
The long winds blow, a tree lies low
That was an old friend:
The winter snow, the summer's glow—
Shall these things have an end?

When I was young I used to think
I should not taste of death;
And now I faint to reach the brink,
And grudge my every breath
That streameth to the utter air
Leaving me to my tears
And outlook bare, with eyes astare
Upon the creeping years.

[Pg 16]

v

That little old house that seems to stoop
Yellow under thatch,
Like a three-sided chicken-coop,
Where, if you watch,
You'll see the starlings go and come
All a spring morn—
Half of that is my old home
Where I was born.

One half a little old cottage
The five of us had,
Five tall sisters in a cage
With our Mother and Dad.
Alice she was the eldest one,
Then Mary, and then me,
And then Fanny, and little Joan,
The last-born was she.

Never a boy that liv'd to grow
Did our mother carry;
She us'd to wonder how she'd do
With five great girls to marry.
But once I heard her say to Dad,
A chain of pretty girls
Made out her neck the comelier clad
Than diamonds or pearls.

[Pg 17]

vi

How we did do on Father's money
Is more than I can tell:
There was the money from the honey,
And Mother's work as well;
For she did work with no more rest
Than the buzzing bees,
And the sight I knew and lov'd the best
Was Mother on her knees.

When we were fed and clean for school,
Out Mother goes,
Rinsing, rubbing, her hands full
Of other people's clothes.

If there's one thought above another
Sets my heart singing,
It's thinking of my little sweet Mother,
Her arms full of linen.

And yet she rul'd her house and all
Us girls within it;
There was no meal but we could fall
To it at the minute;
Thing there was none, said, thought or done,
But she must know it,
Nor any errand to be run
But she made us go it.

She with her anxious, watchful glance,
Blue under her glasses,
Was meat and drink and providence
To us five lasses.
Out she fetcht from hidden stores
White frocks for Sundays,
And always nice clean pinafores
Against school, Mondays.
[Pg 18]
She and Dad were little people,
But most of us were tall,
And I shot up like Chichester steeple;
Fan, she was small.
You never saw a kinder face
Or met with bluer eyes:
If ever there was a kissing-case
On her mouth it lies.

vii

When I was old enough for skipping
My school days began;
By Mary's side you'd see me tripping—
I was baby then.
A B C and One-two-three
Were just so much Greek;
But I could read, it seems to me,
As soon as I could speak.

Before I knew how fast I grew
I was the tallest there;
Before my time was two-thirds thro'
I must plait my hair;
Before our Alice took a place
And walkt beside her fancy,
I had on my first pair of stays
And saw myself Miss Nancy.
[Pg 19]
And then goodbye to form and desk
And sudden floods of noise
When fifteen minutes' fun and frisk
Make happy girls and boys.
As shrill as swifts in upper air
Was our young shrillness:
'Twas joy of life, 'twas strength to fare
Broke the morning stillness.

I see us flit, as here I sit
With wet-fring'd eyes,
And never rime or reason to it—
Like a maze of flies!
The boys would jump and catch your shoulder
Just for the fun of it—
They tease you worse as you grow older
Because you want none of it.

I hear them call their saucy names—
Mine was Maypole Nance;
I see our windy bickering games,

Half like a dance;
The opening and closing ring
Of pinafored girls,
And the wind that makes the cheek to sting
Blowing back their curls!

There in the midst is Sally Waters,
As it might be I,
With the idle song of Sons and Daughters
Drifting out and by
Sons and daughters! Break, break,
Heart, if you can—
How have they taught us treat sons and daughters
Since I began?

[Pg 20]

viii

There is a bank that always gets
The noon sun full;
There we'd hunt for violets
After morning school.
White and blue we hunted them
In the moss, and gave them,
Dropping-tir'd and short in stem,
To Mother. She must have them.

Primrose-mornings in the copse,
Autumn berrying
Where the dew for ever stops,
And the serrying,
Clinging shrouds of gossamers
Glue your eyes together;
Gleaning after harvesters

In the mild blue weather—

Life so full of bud and blossom,
Fallen like a tree!
Who gave me a woman's bosom—
And who has robb'd me?

[Pg 21]

III

i

When from the folds the shepherd comes
At the shut of day,
The fires are lit in valley homes,
The smoke blue and grey—
So still, so still!—hangs o'er the thatch;
So still the night falls,
My love might know me at the latch
By my heart-calls.

And hear you me, my love, this night
Where Grief and I are set?
And look you for the beacon light,
And can you see it yet?
Or is the sod too deep, my love,
Which they piled over you?
Or are you bound in sleep, my love,
Lying in the dew?

ii

When I was done with schooling days,
Turn'd sixteen,
My mother found me in a place
My own bread to win.
I had not been a month in place,
A month from the start,
When there show'd grace upon my face
That smote a man's heart.
[Pg 22]
Tho' I was young and full of play,
As full as a kitten,
I knew to reckon to a day
When his heart was smitten.
You'll pick my logic all to holes,
But here's my wonder:
It is that God should knit two souls,
And men tear them asunder.

For we were knit, no doubt of it,
I as well as he;
I peered in glass, my eyes were lit
After he'd lookt at me.
I knew not why my heart was glad,
Or why it leapt, but so 'tis,
The sharpest, sweetest pang I've had
Was when he took notice.

And 'tis not favour makes a lad
To a girl's mind,
But 'tis himself makes good of bad,
Or her stone-blind.
And men may cheer at tales of wars,
But every girl knows
What makes her eyes to shine like stars

And her face a rose.

iii

No word he said, but turned his head
After he'd lookt at me;
I coloured up a burning red,
Setting the cloth for tea.
The board was spread with cakes and bread
For farmer in his sleeves,
For mistress and the shepherd Ted;
They talkt of hogs and theaves—
[Pg 23]
But nothing ate I where I sat,
So bashful as I was,
But kept my eyes upon my plate
And pray'd the minutes pass.
Tic-toc, tic-toc from great old clock,
The long hand did creep;
And every stroke in my heart woke
Nature out of her sleep.

So once, they tell, did Gabriel
Name a young Maid
For honour and a miracle,
And few words she said;
But things have changed a wondrous deal
Since she was nam'd,
If to her room she did not steal
As if she were asham'd;

And there upon her bed to sit
Astare, as I guess,
Watching her fingers weave and knit,
Bedded in her dress,

A-thinking thoughts in her young mind
Too wild for tears to gain,
As when the roaring North-West wind
Gives no time to the rain.

[Pg 24]

iv

Give thanks, you maids, that there's your work
To keep your heart and head
From thoughts that lurk in them who shirk
Their daily round to tread.
But she goes bold who feels the hold
And colour of her love
Laid on her task like water-gold
From the lit sky above.

v

I rose with early morning light,
The meadows grey with rime,
To set the kitchen fire, and dight
The room for breakfast-time;
Or make the beds, or rinse and scour,
And all the while
A singing heart, a face aflower,
And secret smile.

So 'twas with me week in, week out,
And no more to be said;

A moment's look, a hint of doubt,
A half-turn of the head.
I had my hands as full as full,
And full of work was he—
But I learn'd in another school
After he'd lookt at me.

[Pg 25]

vi

In summer time of flowers and bees
And flies on the pane,
Before the sun could gild the trees
Or set afire the vane,
Down I must go upon my knees,
Or ply the showering mop;
Then feed the chicken, ducks and geese,
And milk the last drop.

On winter mornings dark and hard,
White from aching bed,
There were the huddled fowls in yard
All to be fed.
My frozen breath stream'd from my lips,
The cows were hid in steam;
I lost sense of my finger-tips
And milkt in a dream.

My drowsy cheek fast to her side,
The pail below my arm,
My thought leapt what might me betide,
And soon I was warm.
For that gave me a beating heart
And made me hot thro',

As when you reckon, with a start,
Someone speaks of you.

vii

And all my years of farm-service
There was no dismay,
But men and maids knew nought amiss
With their work or play;
But grew amain like tree or beast,
Labouring out their lives
Till sap and milk fill'd spine and breast,
And ripen'd men and wives.
[Pg 26]
What call had we to think of war,
We growing things?
What need had we to reckon o'er
Misdoubts or threatenings?
A soldier-lad in his red coat
Show'd up then as he past
Like a lamplighted fishing-boat
Lonely in the vast.

An aeroplane in middle sky
Might bring us to our doors,
To see her like a dragon-fly
Droning as she soars.
Long before you see her come
You can hear her throbbing,
Far, far away like a distant drum,
Near, like a thresher sobbing.

Ah, in those days of wonderment,
Wonder and delight,
No thought we spent what murder meant,

Horror in the night;
Or how a hidden dreadful plan
Like a fingering weed
Was growing up in the mind of man
From a fungus-seed!

[Pg 27]

IV

i

Out of the clear how shrewdly blows
The North-West wind!
Free as he goes, how brave he shows,
The sun seems blind!
The shadows fleet upon the grass
Where the kestrels hover—
What leagues of sorrow they must pass
Before they shroud my lover!

Half-naked now, confronting cold,
The tall trees shiver,
Each with its pool of pallid gold
Draining down to the river.
'Tis now when fret of winter wet
Warns the year she is old,
And she casts robe and coronet,
That I would loosen hold.

ii

Our lives creep on to change at last,
And change is sudden coming;
Rooted you see yourself and fast,
And then be sent roaming.
When I was come to twenty years,
Home for a spell,
Mother she brought a flush of tears
With what she had to tell.
[Pg 28]
There was a fine new place for me
Forty miles away—
And where my dream of what might be
One fine day?
The farmer's wife she kiss'd me kindly
When I was paid;
But Ted and I said Goodbye blindly,
And no more said.

No word between us of the thought
That fill'd four years,
No fond look caught by eyes well taught,
Tho' thick with tears!
'Twas Goodbye, Nance, and Goodbye, Ted,
And just a clasp of the hand:
Maybe I'll write, he might have said
For me to understand.

But poor people have need to work
Whether merry or sad,
Whatever groping thought do lurk,
Whatever dreams they've had!
I went my way and he kept his,
I to the county town,
He in a row of cottages

Below the hump-backt down.

iii

A town-bred girl, her hair in curl
And apron edged with lace,
She took me in, my head awhirl,
To my new place.
And there the five of us must hive
In that warm shutter'd house,
And keep our honesty alive
With none to counsel us.
[Pg 29]
The master and the mistresses,
What were they but strangers?
'Twas no part of their businesses
To think of servants' dangers.
They sneer at us, and we at them,
Life sunders where the stairs are:
But are the things that they condemn
In us much worse than theirs are?

iv

'Twas busy now I had to be,
And keep myself neat,
Dress in my new black gown by tea,
And streamer'd cap to it.
The brisk young men were plenty enough,
And talk about them plenty
Among us maids! No other stuff

Contents the tongue at twenty.

But Mother's words came back to me,
Told when I was little:
Mind you, the tongue's your only key,
And what it guards is brittle.
Love is the best; let go the rest,
But hold him by the wing
Until he's plumaged for the test—
Then let him soar and sing.
[Pg 30]
I took no harm of all their talk—
All talkt the same—
Tho' more than one askt me to walk
When my Sunday came;
But I held fast the dream I'd had
In the old farm,
And saw myself beside my lad,
My hand on his arm.

V

A year went on, and twenty-one
Saw me discarded.
They laught at me for constancy
Ne'er to be rewarded.
Then came a warm, still day of May
And brought me a letter.
I blusht so red, the cook she said,
Lucky man to get her!

At half-past three he came for me;
I dared not speak;
But there was all he need to see
Flaming in my cheek.

What better has the best of us
If kind Heaven grant her
A glowing hearth, a little house,
And a good man to want her?
[Pg 31]
In the soft shrouding clinging mist
His strong arms held me.
Our lips kept tryst, and long we kiss'd;
His great love fill'd me.
Sweet is the warmth of summer weather,
But the best fire I know
Is of two pair of lips together,
Two hearts in one glow.

His love he told, that made me bold
To look at him fairly,
And see the burning blush take hold
And colour him up rarely.
Within his ply though caught was I,
I backt a saucy head:
"Oh, I was shy a year gone by—
Your turn now," I said.

vi

Now would you prove the man I love
As I saw him then?
He was of them who're slow to move,
One of your still men;
One of your men self-communing
Who see sheep on a hill,
Ships out at sea or birds a-wing
Where you see *nil*.

And what they see they seldom say,
Holding speech to be vain;
And yet so kin to earth are they
They smell the coming rain.
The earth can teach them without speech,
They know as they are known—
Why should they preach to the out-of-reach,
Or counsel Nature's own?
[Pg 32]
He never was a man to talk,
He was too wise;
But things he'd see out on his walk
Would blind another's eyes.
But when it came to speak about them
'Twas another thing.
He'd say, "What use is it to shout them?
I want to sing!"

A smallish head, with jet-black hair
And eyes grey-blue,
You felt when'er he lookt you fair
That he must be true;
And when he smil'd his dear and shy way
Sidelong his mouth,
I always thought the sun fell my way
And the wind South.

So I possest the knowledge blest
That Love had held him fast
Since the day our eyes confest,
The first time and the last.
"Since then," he said, "I never durst
Look at you at all,
For fear you'd see the hunger and thirst
That kept me like a thrall.

[Pg 33]

vii

"'Twas when you went away and left
Me and pain alone,
By fortune's theft I stood bereft
Of all I'd counted on—
And this also, I ne'er could go
On my shepherd life,
Without I had the grace to woo
You my loving wife.

"There was a fate, I do believe,
Call'd us together;
God visit me when'er you grieve
Taking on my tether!
But if we share with every creature
That is quick and dead
The call of nature unto nature,
Then we two should wed.

"You are a beauty bred and born,
As any one can see;
You walk the world as if in scorn
Of riches or degree.
Your eyes call home the soft green tone
Of the fainting sky
When the eve-star keeps watch alone,
And the summer is nigh.
[Pg 34]
"But 'tis your grave and constant mind
Beckon'd me to you,
Too good, too sweet, too fond, too kind,
For me to be untrue.
So trust me, lass, I'll not be false
While I do live,
For we two go where Nature calls,

As I believe."

viii

Trust! Oh, I could have sunk to ground
And lain under his feet!
To have his praise was like a wound,
Throbbing and deadly sweet;
A wound that lets the welling blood
Ebb from the vein,
Merging the hurt in drowsihood,
And hushing down the pain.

High destiny of Nature's calling,
Foil'd and frustrate!
Just then the evil tide was crawling
To drown love in hate.

[Pg 35]

V

i

The meadows wear a cloth of gold,
The trees wear green;
Upon the down in dimpled fold
The white lambs glean;

Deep blue the skyey canopy,
Soft the wind's fan:
Behold the earth as it might be
If man lov'd man!

Summer is soon; the next new moon
Will see the yellowing wheat;
Then will be harvest, Earth's high boon
To them that work for it.
The reapers swink, the heat-waves blink
Across the drowsy fen—
Now let hearts shrink from scythes that drink
The blood of young men!

ii

As I stood at my open door
I caught a flying word:
Two strangers past, "Then that means war——"
That was what I heard.
'Twas ten o'clock, a summer's day,
My love on the hill.
"Then that means war," I heard them say,
And my heart stood still.
[Pg 36]
Life had been fair as I stood there,
Eight weeks a bride;
All of me laid warm and bare
To my true love's side!
Oh, who should dream of dark to-morrows
And lonely weeping
Whose steadfast joys and passing sorrows
Lay in such a keeping?

There blew a chill wind from the hill
Like a sea-breath;
I shiver'd and a taint of ill
Brought news of death.
I blinkt my eyes as who should try
To see what is to fear;
The sun still shone high in the sky,
But no warmth there.

Then far away I saw the sea
A rippling golden sheet,
And courage flowed again in me—
What foe could break thro' it?
And all about the fields and hedges,
There when I was born,
The river slipping through the sedges,
And the growing corn—

A land of quiet tilth and cote,
Of little woods and streams,
Of gentle skies and clouds afloat,
And swift sun-gleams!
A land where knee-deep cattle keep,
Chewing as they stand;
Of hillsides murmurous with sheep—
That is my native land!
[Pg 37]
They say you never love so dear
As when you are to part;
I know, to see my land so clear
Cut me to the heart.
What vain regrets to have lov'd so ill
What was our all!
What idle vows to love her still
Though she should fall!

At stroke of noon my love came in
Sharpset for his food;
To see him was right sense to win,

And feel safe and good.
I was asham'd my fears to tell
Lest he should think,
"I thought I knew this woman well—
But what makes her shrink?"

iii

The summer went her gracious way
Of sun and lingering eves;
I did my share to win the hay,
The corn stood in sheaves
Ere August month was fairly come;
And when it was here
I knew I carried in my womb
The harvest of my dear.

[Pg 38]

iv

When I was sure I sat down quiet
In the deep shade,
And if my heart was all in riot
I was not afraid.
I did not think, nor say a pray'r,
But lookt straight before me,
And felt that Someone else stood there
With hands held o'er me.

I thought His peace blest my increase;
But then, as it seem'd,
A shadow made my joy to cease,
And the day was dimm'd.
I shiver'd as if one a knife
Should pull forth of the sheath.
I think just then the Lord of Life
Gave way to Him of Death.

As one bestead with gossamer-thread
I pluckt at my eyes
To catch again the glory shed,
The hope, the load, the prize;
But no more hands invisible
Held like a shade o'er me,
And there seem'd little enough to tell
My husband momently.

The long forenoon my thought I held,
And yet all thro' it
The wires all England over shrill'd,
And I never knew it!
In a high muse I nurst my news
All the forenoon,
While England braced her limbs and thews
To a marching tune.

[Pg 39]

V

I serv'd my love, when he came home,
His meal; then on his knee
I told him what I might become,
And he kiss'd me;

Then said, "Indeed, there may be need
Of this little one,
For many a woman's heart must bleed
For wanting of a son.

"Since we awoke, the word is spoke,
And if 'tis still right
That English folk keep faith unbroke,
Then must England fight."
I could not look, nor think, nor ask
What himself would do,
But call'd to task my pride, to bask
In what had warm'd me thro'.

Oh, he was grave and self-possest
Under love's new crown!
He took me in his arms to rest,
And lay my head down
A moment on his shoulder; then
Went steady to his work.
I knew what fate soe'er call'd men
He was none to shirk.
[Pg 40]
Now I must play the helpful wife,
And my new pride
Be little worth to ease the strife
That vext me in the side;
For like a green and aching wound,
Like a throbbing vein
I felt this terror on the ground
Of young men slain.

The swooning summer sun sank low,
And all the dusty air
Held breathlessly beneath his glow,
So tir'd, so quiet and fair,
I would not think that men could live
In such glory a minute,
To hate and grudge, to slay and reive

Poor souls within it.

vi

I heard fond crying in my ears,
Fond and vain regret
For life as it had been ere tears
Made women's eyes wet;
I saw arise the host of stars
And listen'd to their song;
"O we have seen a thousand wars
And woe agelong!

"What are you men, what are you women
But a shifting sand?
The tide of life is overbrimming—
God holds not His hand;
But all the evil with the good
To His mill is grist;
He serves his mood now with man's blood
Who serv'd it once with beast."
[Pg 41]
So sang the stars. That night our love
Burn'd at its holiest;
For aught we knew the same might prove
Our last in the nest.
But from the bed my passion pled,
O God, let us be!
If woman's anguish her bestead,
Then forsake not me!

vii

I dare not trace that watching space
Of days, too short, too long—
Too long to wear a patient face,
Too short to wear a strong.
I us'd to think I'd have him choose
His duty and begone;
And then, No, no, I dare not lose
Him ere he take his son!

Too long, too short the days to wait,
To plan and think and dread;
And happy we whose poor estate
Claims our work for our bread.
Each day I went to scour and scrub
As my mother us'd,
Or stood before the washing-tub
Where the linen sluiced.
[Pg 42]
And so my love with careful hand
And careful eye
Led his white flock about the land;
And I must sigh,
"There's no rebelling in a poor man's dwelling,
The roof stoops to the blast;
And no heart-swelling meets God's compelling,
And what is cast is cast!"

viii

But as the tide crawls to his full
Without your knowing,
Invading rock and filling pool,
Endlessly flowing;

Lo, while you sit and look at it,
Idle, little thinking,
The flood is brimming at your feet,
Lipping there and winking—

The very same the Great War grew;
Like a flowing tide
It spread its channels thro' and thro'
The quiet countryside.
One day you'd stop: a poster up,
And Lord, how it glared!
The next there'd be a very crop,
And not a body stared.

And then the lorries flung along
By ones and twos, and then
In snaky line some twenty strong,
Full of shouting men.
They made me blench with noise and stench,
But more, I do believe,
To know them gaining inch by inch
The earth whereby we live.
[Pg 43]
So faded fast the painted past
Beneath the mist of war;
One could not think life had been cast
In sweet lines before.
There was no list in that red mist
For love or wholesome breath,
But making rage our staple grist
We ground the dust of death.

Our men held talk among themselves,
But said little to we;
And soon they went by tens and twelves
Soldiers to be.
I knew how 'twould be from the first,
I think my heart could tell;
I loved a man who never durst

Not do well.

ix

How young, how gay they marcht away,
All our village boys!
Leaving us women here to pray,
Drowning with their noise
Misdoubt and eager mother-love,
Hungry on the watch,
As if they went to race and shove
In a football match.
[Pg 44]
But my love chose in soberness
Another way, his own;
And God I bless that my distress
Came suddenly down.
A swift November night was falling
In a windless air;
I heard him indoors, heard him calling,
And went, and he was there.

x

He stood still, and his gaze
Was far off, and slow
And quiet the words he says:
"Nancy, I must go."

In my still heart's deep
I gloried in the trust

He handed me to keep,
In his quiet "I must."

No more we said that night,
But sat in the gloom;
We sat without candle-light
In our little room.

Handfast, like girl and boy,
There we sat on,
Hoarding our store of joy
Against he were gone.
[Pg 45]
Handfast, like boy and girl,
And my eyes they did fill;
But my heart was in a whirl
To have him there still.

'Twas when we were abed,
And I against his heart,
That I knew the great dread
It would be to part.

Old sayings, that sounded new,
Sweet, every broken word—
"My Nancy, sweet and true,
My pretty wild bird!"

I let him kiss me, but I
Lay quite still in his arm:
If I had started to cry
God only knew the harm!

And if he thought me cool
'Twould make an easier going;
But *if* he thought me cool
'Twas not for want of knowing.

Towards the twilight gray
When my love was sleeping,
I sat upright to pray,
And heard the sparrows cheeping.
[Pg 46]
It was their fond love-twitter
That broke my prayer down,
Turn'd all my faith bitter,
To set it by their own.

Their love-life to begin,
And mine now—where?
Their nest to win,
Mine soon to be bare!

I lookt forth from my bed
To the cold square of the light—
Unto God I said,
"Show me why men must fight,

"You, Who to each one say,
Love you one another;
You, Who bid women obey
Husbands, and sons their mother;

"You, Who of me require
To love what I cannot see,
Milk and a heart of fire
To nourish what may not be!

"Shall my milk be churn'd into gall,
Or my blood freeze at the fount,
And You make light of it all,
And my love of little account?"
[Pg 47]
Then as I held my throat,
God answer'd me by a bird,
One long flourishing note,

The bravest I ever heard;

And I turn'd where my love lay fast
In his wholesome sleep;
About him my arms I cast
And found grace to weep.

He would do what was right,
As I knew very well—
Yes, but who made them fight,
And turn'd our heaven to hell?

The more I listen the sighs,
The mourning and the dearth,
The deeper my heart cries
Over this wounded earth.

[Pg 48]

VI

i

May the good King
That guards like sheep
Kings and shepherds all
Send us quiet sleep!

Shepherds great and small
Has He in hold;
There need no danger

Threaten field or fold.

Lowly in a manger
That King was born
Of maid undefiled
On a winter's morn.

He lay a little child
On His mother's knee;
Three kings out of the East
Came Him to see.

On a mother's breast
Still did He lie:
Said one king to the other,
"Such once was I!"

Then said his brother,
"Even thus, I trow,
Once lay thy simplicity,
But where is that now?"

[Pg 49]

ii

How many a woman's eyes are worn,
Weeping a murder'd son!
How many wish none they had borne
To do as theirs have done!
Who dares to see a mask of hate
And snarling on the face
Which she had pray'd to consecrate
To honour for a space?

This high-flusht lad whom she has known
Since as a new-born child
He lay as soft as thistle-down,
Or like an angel smil'd;
Whom she has seen, a sturdy imp
Tumble bare-breecht at play,
Or nurst to health when, quiet and limp,
Short-breath'd and flusht he lay;

Or shockhead boy, aburst with joy,
Or gawky, ill-at-ease,
All hot and coy, a hobbledehoy
With laces round his knees—
But hers, her own, with eyes that trust
Hers for his better part—
Ah, tiger-lust of War that thrust
A hand to snatch that heart!

She hides her woe, and helps him go,
She sits at home to pray;
He tells her when he met the foe,
But nothing of the way.
She never knows the way, and who
Would know it if she could,
What in his fever-heat he do
Of rage and dust and blood?
[Pg 50]
The lads go by, the colours fly,
Drums rattle, bugles bray;
We only cry, Let mine not die—
No thought for whom he slay.
But woman bares a martyr breast,
And herself points the flame:
Her son, a hero or a beast,
Will never be the same.

iii

When forth my love to duty went
I sought my old home,
My few months' joy over and spent,
And lean years to come.
My mother blinkt her patient eyes;
She said, It was to be.
Was I less temperate or more wise
To question her decree?

Was it for this, our clasp and kiss?
For this end and no other
That I was shapt to have increase,
And call'd to be mother?
Did God make o'er the power to soar
On men, that they should sink?
Did He outpour a flood of war
And leave us on the brink?
[Pg 51]
Was't so He wove the robe of Love,
To mock the lovely earth?
Sees He, above, creation move
To death, not birth?
Go, thou dear head, for God is dead,
And Death is our Lord:
Between us, red, lies in the bed
War, like a naked sword.

iv

O failing heart, accept your part,
And thank the Lord, Who bound

Your labour daily to the mart,
Your service to the ground!
Take to the mart your stricken heart,
Tho' the chaffer graze it;
Shrink not altho' the quick flesh smart—
But meet pain and praise it!

V

He came to see me once again,
Stiffen'd in his new buff:
A few short hours compact of strain,
Too hasty for love;
For Love can never be confin'd,
But asks eternity.
To nurse the lov'd one in the mind
The bond must first be free.
[Pg 52]
And he, he now serv'd otherwhere
And could not be the same;
To all the world my love was there
And answer'd to his name;
But not to me, oh, not to me
The kisses of his lips
Were as of old, but guardedly,
Like sunlight in eclipse.

The moment came, I held him close,
But had no word to say—
Good-bye, sweetheart, Good-bye, Blush Rose:
'Twas his old way.
Then in a hush which seem'd to rock
Me like a leaf about,
I heard the pulsing of the clock,

Counting my dear life out.

And I am here, and you are, where?
While the long hours go by,
And on my eyes the glaze of care,
And in my heart a cry.
Bury my heart deep in the grave
Where all its grace is hid:
What other service should I have
Than tend my lovely dead?

vi

Then waiting, watching, judging news,
Then terror in the night—
I used to start up with the dews
All over me of fright.
I dream'd of him on stormy seas;
Then, in a woodland bare,
I saw my love on hands and knees,
With blood upon his hair.
[Pg 53]
Along the limits of the wood,
A green bank full of holes,
With lichen'd stumps which lean'd or stood
Like crazy channel-poles:
'Twas there I saw my love's drawn face,
A face of paper-white,
Wherein just for a choking space
His eyes shone burning bright;

Then faded, and an eyeless man
He crawled along the wood,
And from his hair a black line ran
And broaden'd into blood.

It was not horror of him wrong'd,
It was not pity mov'd me;
It was, those tortur'd eyes belong'd
To one who'd never lov'd me.

That was my love in face and shape,
That was my love in pain;
But something told me past escape
That not by him I'd lain.
I sat and star'd into the night,
And still most dreadfully
I saw those two eyes burning white
That never had seen me!

[Pg 54]

vii

Upon a wild March morn
My husband went to France;
The day my child was born
His word came to advance.

'Twas on that very day
When my life should be crown'd,
As I lay in, he lay
Broken upon the ground.

For my loss there was gain,
But his precious blood
Was shed to earth like rain
Within the shatter'd wood.

Missing, the paper said,
But my heart said, Nay.

Missing! My man had been dead
Before he went away!

viii

It never throve from the first,
Mother, she seem'd to fear it;
But her words were the worst:
"Nancy, you'll never rear it."

Yet he took to the breast
And I knew the great end
Of women, to give their best,
To spend and to spend.
[Pg 55]
But his great eyes stared
Till he seemed all eyes,
And more than I dared
Meet looks so wise.

Wondering and darkly blue,
Pondering and slow,
They would look you thro' and thro',
Then tire and let you go,

And fall back to vacancy,
As if the poor thing plain'd,
"Why was I not let be,
And what have I gain'd?"

'Twas more than I could bear,
I pray'd that he might die;
And God must have heard my prayer,
For he went with a little sigh:

A flutter, a murmur, a sigh
Lighter than dawn wind—
It was his soft Good-bye;
And all my life lay behind.

I wonder if they were wise,
Those three kings of the East
Who offer'd gifts of price
To the Child on a Girl's breast.
[Pg 56]
But if they were wise, their sons
Have other counsel than they:
The gifts they offer are guns,
And the children's parents they slay.

ix

He went before my load was quicken'd,
And I lay in alone.
He was not there when baby sicken'd,
Nor when it was gone.
I walkt with Mother to the church,
With Mother and Fan,
My hard eyes ever on the search—
Pity me who can!

The grief was bad enough to bear,
So dreadfully to wean it;
But to go home and leave it there,
And he had never seen it—!
It was a thing to thank God for
That home for me was none;
I knew before we reacht the door
That my home life was done.

x

Now limpt or dragg'd about our street
The wounded men in blue,
Trailing the feet which had been fleet,
Or crutching one for two;
Like ghosts of men past out of ken,
Pale and uncertain-eyed,
Whose gaze would flicker out, and then
Come back with hasty pride.
[Pg 57]
What they had seen they never told,
Nor what they had done:
I saw young lads turn'd suddenly old;
I saw the blind in the sun
Look up to pray, as if the blue
Was shapt like a cross.
There came back one my husband knew,
Spoke kindly of my loss.

He told me how my love was dead;
He was not the first!
Broadcast our land the word of dread
Told women the worst.
They say, let love and light be given
So we keep Liberty;
But I say there is no more Heaven
If men must so be free.

xi

Can it be own'd that kings were crown'd,
Consecrate to such evil?

God-appointed, by God anointed
Only to play the devil!
Their men to bind of the tiger kind,
To bind and then to goad,
Blundering, slavering, hot and blind,
On murder's hollow road?
[Pg 58]
If kings are so, then let all go—
Let my dear love cast down
His lovely life, so we lay low
The last to wear a crown.
I'll look upon the steadfast stars,
Patient and true and wise,
And read in them the end of wars,
As in my dead love's eyes.

O Lord of Life, for whom this earth
Should image back Thy thought,
Wherein the mystery of birth
In Love like Thine be wrought,
If pity stands with Thy commands,
Grant a short breathing-space
Ere men hold up their bloody hands
Before Thy awful face.

[Pg 59]

[Pg 60]

Note

This poem is dramatic, and I am not to be supposed answerable for all that it expresses; nevertheless I think that my own convictions about aggressive war are very much those of my Village Wife. Of defensive war, of war to save the lives of our children, of war to save humanity itself, there cannot be two sane opinions: that is a pious duty forced upon us; but it becomes every day more inconceivable to me how men can engage in the other kind of war, and how, in particular, a people so provident as the German people could have hoodwinked themselves into believing that they could be better off by such a monstrous means as warfare has now become. They had behind them the experience of the Russians and Japanese; they had all about them the evidences of their forty years' commercial activity; they must have known, or at least their governors must have known, what kind of results might be looked for from modern armament—and yet they dared risk the dereliction of human morality, the cutting off of a generation of men, and their own national bankruptcy. Whether it was the madness of lust, or of pride, or of fear, it was a madness which has procured the greatest disaster of recorded time, and revealed a criminal folly in themselves which it will take more than two generations to efface. Indeed, German blood-lust will become one of the standing legends of History.

The Village Wife knows nothing of the Germans, however, and her reproaches strike at the heart of Mankind. So long as Mankind [Pg 61] looks upon aggressive war as a reasonable, if ultimate, appeal, her reproaches will have force, and be deserved. They, or something like them (with the sanction of inspiration upon them) will, I believe, be the means of our redemption. As human nature still actually is, no League of Nations conceivable to us will be able to save us from war. Rend your hearts and not your armaments. Let us learn to look War in the face, and while the blood is cold, so that we may know what we are meaning to do. Let us put a moral taboo upon it, such as we have put upon parricide, or incest, or cannibalism. For certain, in those matters, the reason has put a sanction on the conscience. So will it in the matter of aggressive war. Side by side with that, as we now see, we must change the governance of nations. If those who do a nation's work are given their due share of that nation's government, war I firmly believe, will become a dark memory, a blotted cloud upon a past age. "Hundreds of years ago," it will one day be said to some wondering child, "men hired men to murder each other for the sake of their religion or their commerce. This they had done for thousands of years until at last, in the most dreadful of their wars, they killed or maimed a whole generation in the space of about four years. Then it was that men saw what they had been doing, and for a while the world was shamed, silent. That time of silence was long enough to turn the hearts of men."

I have put into the mouth of my Village Wife thoughts which she may never have formulated, but which, I am very sure, lie in her heart, too deep for any utterance but that of tears. If I know anything of village people I know this, that they shape their lives according to Nature, and are outraged to the root of their being by the frustration of Nature's laws and the stultification of man's function in the scheme of things. What the function of man is, what the power, what the dignity have been well paraphrased in these words:

[Pg 62]

"'Neither a fixed abode, nor a form in thine own likeness, nor any gift peculiar to thyself alone, have we given thee, O Adam, in order that what abode, what likeness, what gifts thou shalt choose may be thine to have and to possess. The nature allotted to all other creatures, within laws appointed by ourselves, restrains them. Thou, restrained by no narrow bounds, according to thy own free will, in whose power we have placed thee, shalt define thy nature for thyself. We have set thee midmost the world, that thence thou mightest more conveniently survey whatsoever is in the world. Nor have we made thee either heavenly or earthly, mortal or immortal, to the end that thou, being, as it were, thy own free maker and moulder, shouldst fashion thyself in what form may like thee best. Thou shalt have power to decline unto the lower or brute creatures. Thou shalt have power to be reborn unto the higher or divine, according to the sentence of thy intellect.' Thus to Man, at his birth, the Father gave seeds of all variety and germs of every form of life."

That is near enough to the Nature of Man for present purposes.

"Teach us man's worth, that we may know it,
Who, being alone in power to lift
Above his nature, sinks below it!"

Broadchalke, *7th July*, 1918. [Pg 63]